THE ALIEN'S CONFLICT

GRACE KENSINGTON

1

Pyra drew his tiny son closer to his body, resting him directly over his heart and tucking his head so that he could envelope him completely and draw in a breath of his scent. Eden's words had struck him deeply and he couldn't shake the thoughts that they had inspired in his mind. His mate had always spoken of the man who had been her boss on Earth and sent her on the scientific expedition to Uoria with a sense of disgust and anger, but he had never heard the level of fear and apprehension in her voice that he did then as she revealed that she thought that Ryan was capable of far more than anyone had ever imagined. She stared at Lysander as she said it as if she were revealing something that she had held within her for so long but was only now willing to put a voice to because of the fragile baby that was now in the world, vulnerable to everything and needing the protection of his parents.

"What do you think that he could do?" Pyra asked, trying to keep his voice as calm and steady as he could so that he wouldn't frighten his mate any more than she already was.

The last several weeks had been incredibly illuminating

to the lead warrior of the Denynso. He had left the compound for the first time in his life with determination to find out what else lived on his beloved planet, identify any threats that might exist, and find ways to resolve them so that they could not harm the baby that was not yet born at that time. What he thought would be a simple journey had turned into something complex and horrifying, showing him not just the creatures that lived on that planet and what threats they held, but also the hidden threats that he never thought he would encounter again, and could never have imagined existed. What was just as, and possibly even more horrifying than the creatures he had found and what he had learned about the history of the planet was how much he had changed after learning everything.

Pyra, like all Denynso warriors, confronted threats with aggression, violence, and fury. This was what had earned them the reputation as being the most fearsome, powerful, and effective warriors in the galaxy. As he learned about the Covra and what they did to the people of the settlement, and then the Mikana and their unexpected disturbing connection to the Klimnu that he thought they had eliminated in that last terrifying battle, a change came over Pyra that was unlike anything that he had ever experienced. He felt a level of anger, disgust, and vicious desire for vengeance that he had never felt.

In an instant he went from wanting to help the humans who had been locked by the Covra and being willing to accept the help of the strange but beautiful people from the nearby kingdom that had once maintained good relations with the settlement to wanting to destroy and eliminate all of the Mikana and anyone who had stood in his way. In them he saw not just the Klimnu that had tormented his kind for years and been the cause of pain, fear, and death for as long as he could remember, torturing not just the Denynso warriors who engaged in battle with them, but also the human women who came to the planet and became the mates of several of the Denynso men, but as a deeply disturbing form of betrayal from his planet.

The Mikana were beautiful, seemingly kind creatures who had immediately welcomed Pyra into their kingdom and offered their assistance when he told them what they were facing with the people of the settlement and the Covra. He had trusted them, relied on them to help him protect the humans of the settlement as well as the warriors and themselves. Soon, though, this trust began to unravel as he learned of the secrets that their leader, Rey, had been withholding and the truth behind their lovely faces and helpful hands came to light.

He had begun to feel wary of them when he found out that Rey had lied to him when he told him that his kind had not had contact with the Covra. They had, in fact, been locked in aggressive conflict with the Covra well before the humans that eventually built the settlement even arrived on the planet. It had been them who had built the prison where the Covra held them captive and where eventually the Klimnu imprisoned and tortured both Leia and Elianna. Though it had made him angry that Rey had willingly lied to him, he could understand the unwillingness to talk about a period of his kind's history that was both horrifying and embarrassing. Rey hadn't meant any harm by not telling Pyra about the conflict and had been forthcoming in telling the truth when it became evident that the information was important to them understanding the humans that turned out to be an assumed lost expedition from Earth called Project Nyx 23.

When the young Mikana who had fallen for the new

human woman who had arrived on the compound after the men had left, Maxim, revealed the reaction that his skin had to some flowers outside of the settlement, however, any sense that he could trust these people, or that they could offer any good to the efforts and existence of the Denynso disappeared. The instant he saw the slimy white change of Maxim's skin, he knew what had happened to the group of the Mikana that Rey said had split off from the rest after the conflict with the Covra ended. They had not just gone off onto the planet with goals of taking over and disappeared. They had become the Klimnu.

As soon as he came to this realization, Pyra felt the level of hatred and disgust toward those creatures that still lingered inside him even after weeks had passed since the final battle, he felt a new level of intensity and voracity that seemed to burn away every bit of compassion and reason within him. If a species that appeared so beautiful and so kind could actually be hiding the capacity for the greatest level of evil and cruelty that Pyra had ever seen behind their lovely faces and gentle words, there was absolutely nothing on the planet that was safe. He couldn't trust or believe in anything. The world around him suddenly went from a place in which he felt dominant and strong, where he felt confident that he would be able to protect his child and raise him well, to a place where the seemingly most innocent and trustworthy of species could turn into a loathsome enemy in a moment.

He had left the compound knowing that he would likely encounter species that he had never seen and may even uncover threats and challenges that would force his warriors to fight and to come up with strategies to protect the rest of the compound now and well into the future. Never had he thought, however, that he would not be able to decipher these threats or that they would appear suddenly and without warning after he had already entrusted them and allowed them in close to him and the rest of those who he was duty-bound to lead and protect. The realization that he was no longer in absolute control and had been misled, even if unknowingly, was at once terrifying and infuriating to Pyra. He was accustomed to being a leader that never stepped down and never shied away from any sort of danger or threat. He was accustomed to being the one that knew when their aggressiveness was needed and creating strategies that kept him in as much control over the situation as was possible.

In those first moments of realizing that all of his beliefs about their defeat of the Klimnu and everything that he thought he knew about the Mikana were completely wrong, something within him had turned like a switch and he was filled with a blazing fury that drove him to capture the entirety of the group of Mikana who had come with him to the settlement, and promised death on them. When Maxim escaped with the help of Ivy and they fled onto the planet only to encounter Pyra again as they made their way through the ruins of the Nyx 23 crash site, he had nearly struck down the young man himself.

It had taken Rain, Ivy, Loralia, and George turning against him amongst the broken, disintegrating pieces of the ship that were being reclaimed by the plants of the planet to force Pyra to realize he didn't have total dominion over all of them, and that he couldn't make the final decision of their life or death. He had to rely on the guidance of his king to tell him what he should do about these creatures. He had been positive that Creia would agree with him and authorize the elimination of the Mikana and, therefore, the final and complete elimination of all future threat of the Klimnu.

After all his father and king had been the one who had been the focus of the beginning war between the Denynso and the Klimnu. It had been Creia's decision not to help those who had first come into contact with the flowers and started to experience the gruesome transformation that had fueled the epic hatred of the Denynso by the Klimnu and the vow of those creatures to not only destroy the warrior race and take over the planet, but to utilize their anger, aggression, and, finally, their blood to make them the most powerful and formidable species that had ever existed.

He was so certain that Creia was going to side with him that Pyra had even permitted the release of Rey from the meeting hall where he had quarantined the rest of the Mikana so that he could come along with them on their journey back to the compound. Having their leader there would be even more influence to Creia and would ensure that there was no argument when he returned to the settlement and then to the kingdom to follow through with the elimination.

When they met with Creia, however, the king had admitted that he himself had been withholding secrets about the origins of the Denynso and when they had come to live on this compound. He had revealed for the first time that they had once inhabited a land on the other side of the rock ledges where none of the Denynso ever ventured, and he had brought them there, allowing them to look out over the devastation caused by those who had confronted the Denynso trying to either become their allies or conquer them and take over their land, and had encountered only defiance. On the top of that rock ledge is where Eden had given birth to Lysander, aided by Rey. As Pyra had watched the leader of the species that he was so ready to destroy without a second thought so carefully and gently tend to his mate and ensure that his son was brought into the world safely, Pyra truly realized the extent of the darkness that had built within him.

The thought frightened and sickened him even now as he cradled that baby to his chest and remembered falling to his knees in front of Creia to ask for forgiveness for what he had done. It terrified him that he could reach that level of cruelty and disregard for life, and it occurred to him that if he was able to fall victim to those thoughts and feelings, then others could as well. He knew that he had failed all those who followed him and could have failed his own son, but through that disturbing transformation he had also illuminated the realities of the world around him. Him feeling capable of that level of destruction meant that he had to protect his son, and all others, from the possibility that someone else could feel that way as well.

2

———

Eden could hear the emotion in her mate's voice as he asked her what she thought Ryan was capable of doing. She wished that there was a way she could tell him what she was thinking without frightening him or inspiring the aggression in him that she heard he had exhibited when he was out of the compound. She had known from the time that she met him that he had a short temper and was prone to anger and violence, but she had a difficult time envisioning what the others had told her had happened when they were on the settlement.

She watched him cuddle Lysander protectively and felt her heart squeeze. Almost as soon as she stepped off of the shuttle onto Uoria for the first time she had made the decision that she was going to put Ryan and everything that she had been through with him behind her. From then she had done everything she could to not think about him or the way he had treated her. Being with Pyra and concentrating on her pregnancy had helped her to rid her mind of the horrible thoughts of him and the nightmares that she had for weeks before her voyage. Now that her child had been born, however, the thoughts were creeping back in and she found herself worrying about what could be waiting outside of the compound.

"Eden?" Pyra said, looking at her sternly. "What do you think that he is capable of doing?"

"I don't know for certain, Pyra. It's not like he ever told me about the horrible things that he was going to do. All I know is the way that he made me feel and the way that his eyes looked. There was something there that I can't really describe. It was something deeper than just his arrogance and his complete disdain for other people. I hope that I don't have to see him while we're there."

"What do you mean you hope that you don't have to see him while you're there? You aren't going to Earth."

Eden looked up at Pyra sharply. Her mate was staring at her with his jaw set, his massive hand stroking Lysander's back with a gentle touch that stood in stark contrast to the intensity on his face.

"Of course I am," she protested. "I'm in Samira's wedding."

"Absolutely not."

"Excuse me?"

"You heard me, Eden. You are absolutely not going. You are staying right here with Lysander and taking care of him while we are on Earth. I'm sure that Samira will understand."

"Samira isn't going to have anything to understand because I am going."

Eden spoke the words slowly and clearly, making sure that he heard and understood each of them.

"Eden, I'm not arguing with you about this. You just gave birth. You need to stay here to heal and get back to normal, and he needs to be here so that he'll be safe. Traveling for days in the shuttle and then being on a new planet just isn't something you can do right now."

"Earth isn't a new planet for me, Pyra. I know that planet far better than I know Uoria, but that's not the point. The point is that I want to go back and see the people I left behind. There aren't many people that I really care about, but those who I do have I want to introduce to you and to Lysander. I want to show them that I am doing well and that I found a new life."

"Are you sure that you don't want to just go back and stay?"

Eden sighed, letting her head hang so that she could massage her temples to ease the tension that was building there.

"Please don't go back into that, Pyra. We've had that discussion already. We went through all of that. I don't want to run away back to Earth. I just want resolution. You have no idea what it was like to just walk away. I don't regret it. Not for a second. I love you more than I could ever tell you and I am completely devoted to my life here on Uoria, but that doesn't mean that I am just going to pretend that my life on Earth never happened. I can honestly tell you that I thought it wasn't going to bother me to be here and never even think about that life again. I thought that I would be able to just carry on without thinking about it or missing it at all. Now that Lysander is here, though, I am realizing how important going back there is to me."

"But why?" Pyra asked, carrying the baby across the room toward his crib. "Why do you need to go back there? You are Denynso now. This is your home and your people."

"I know, Pyra. I know that I'm Denynso, but that doesn't mean that I wasn't once human and that there isn't some human in Lysander. Everyone around me is finding out more about who they are and the history of their kind. Even you have learned more about the clan and how they came to live here on this compound. You can see how much it means to the rest of the clan and to Loralia. Don't you want that for Lysander? Your son deserves to know who he is and where he comes from. Even if he spends his life here and only identifies with the Denynso as he grows up, he should still know the planet where his mother was born and how she came here. You don't know what he's going to want when he's an adult. By then the relations between the Denynso and Earth will be far better. It will likely be common to travel back and forth between the planets and there may even be Denynso settlements on Earth."

"You think that my son will want to leave Uoria?"

"I don't know, Pyra, but neither do you, and it's not our job to tell him who to be or want to want. Our job is to make sure that he has all of the opportunities that he can possibly have and that means teaching him from right now what is beyond the compound."

Pyra tenderly lowered his sleeping infant into the crib and Eden watched him rest his hand lightly on Lysander's belly for a moment as if finding comfort in the rise and fall of his belly as he breathed.

"I don't want him to be in danger, Eden. I don't want either of you to be in danger."

"You must know by now that hiding from the danger doesn't mean that it isn't there. Things are changing. They've been changing. The threats that exist out in the universe are not going to stop existing and they aren't going to stop coming to Uoria. The Denynso have left the compound. You know now about the dangers that are out there, but they know about you, too, and they know more about your vulnerabilities than ever before. You can protect your son from a lot of things, but you aren't going to be able to protect him from everything forever. He has to live."

Pyra turned to her, his glowing orange eyes filled with emotion. He crossed to her and opened his massive arms to her. Eden stepped into them and allowed her mate to curl her against him. Being enveloped by his body was comforting and she allowed herself to relax into him. Having him away from her for so long at the end of her pregnancy had been incredibly difficult. She never could have imagined the devotion that she would have felt for this man, the level of adoration and attachment that she would feel even after knowing him for just a matter of a few days. That passion grew exponentially the longer they were together, and when he was away from her it was as if a part of her heart had actually gone with him. She ached for him in a way that she never could have imagined was possible, and now that he was home again she finally felt like she was complete.

She felt Pyra rest a kiss to the top of her head and she smiled.

"Alright, Eden," he said softly.

She could hear the resignation in his voice. She knew that he hated the words that were coming out of his mouth and that he almost didn't want her to hear them so that he wouldn't have to follow through with them, but that he understood what she had said to him.

"Alright?" she asked.

"Alright. We'll all go. As much as I wish that you didn't go through anything that you went through when you were still on Earth, I will never be able to change how you came to be on Uoria or to be with me. Lysander deserves to know both sides of his heritage. To be honest, I don't want to leave you again. It was horrible being away from you for that time and I was just outside of the compound. I can't imagine how hard it would be to be on a completely different planet from you and from the baby."

"I never want to be anywhere but with you."

"I also don't want to be like my father," Pyra said after a pause.

The words struck Eden and she stepped back to look up into Pyra's face.

"What do you mean?"

"Creia has spent his entire time as king hiding things from the entire clan, and that means hiding things from his children."

"I don't think I've ever heard you refer to yourself as his child," Eden said.

Even though she had known since early on in her time on the planet that many of the impressive warriors in the clan were in fact the children of the king and queen, it was very rare that the relationship was ever mentioned. Creia and Theia interacted with all of them in much the same way and they all referred to the monarchs by their first names or by formal titles. It wasn't that they didn't have the familial love that she had for her son, it was simply a part of the structure of the clan and how they operated within the roles they were duty-bound to uphold.

"I know," Pyra said. "But after finding out that he has kept so much from us and let us believe so many things about the origins of our kind that aren't true, it's hard to think of anything but being betrayed by my father. It's almost like I feel like he should have told us. Even if he wasn't going to tell the rest of the clan, even the rest of the warriors, he could have told my brothers and me. He could have let us know who we really are and how he came to be king. One day there will be a new king and it doesn't seem fair that he was willing to just let the new one take over without knowing everything that he knows."

"Do you think that you will be king one day, Pyra?"

"I don't know. But whether I am or not, Lysander is not going to grow up wondering who he is. Even if that means he might someday want to leave Uoria and live on Earth, which is a decision that I'm going to have to let him make. I can't shield him from everything. You made the choice to come here and to stay here with me. I wouldn't have wanted someone else trying to steer you away from that, so I'm going to have to start preparing myself now to not make decisions for him.

3

"It's so strange," George said, running his hand along Zsilvia's ribs and down into the dip of her waist.

"What is?" Zsilvia asked.

She was lying beside him on their bed, relieved after a particularly boisterous night at the hall to be in the quiet of the home that they had been sharing since returning from their journey. She enjoyed being with the others in the banquet hall, eating and talking, finally feeling relaxed after the hardships of the journey had come to an end, but after having spent so much time traveling and in unfamiliar surroundings, she had longed for more time just with her mate in the privacy of their home. She wanted to lie there beside him, look into his eyes, and be able to enjoy the space that they shared without having to feel like they were always being watched.

George's hand moved onto her hip and she lifted it slightly so that she could press into his touch. Even the simplest of touches from him were thrilling to her. She had waited for so long and had lost hope of ever finding a mate of her own to love. George had come along so unexpectedly and though she had fought hard against what she knew she felt from the moment that she met him, she had finally allowed herself to fall and had tumbled fully, completely, and unendingly in love with him. Having waited so long for him seemed to make every moment with him even more precious and she savored each second that she had to look at him, touch him, and fill her lungs with the scent of him.

"It's strange that I left Earth thinking that I was going to come here, be here on the compound for about six months, and then go back to Earth and maybe teach a seminar at the university about all of the wonderful thing that I discovered while I was on Uoria. Now here I am less than two months later getting ready to go back to Earth without having done a single one of the studies that I had actually planned."

She nuzzled closer to him and brushed the tip of her nose against his.

"And all of those wonderful things that you were going to discover here?"

George ran his hand from her hip back over her waist and onto the side of her breast. His thumb dipped down to stroke across her nipple through her shirt and she immediately felt it tighten at the sensation.

"I won't be sharing the wonderful thing that I discovered here with anybody," he said, bringing his hand to the front of her shirt to release the row of ties down the front, "much less teaching it to a seminar of university students."

George lowered his head and brought his mouth to one of her breasts. Zsilvia gasped at the feeling of his tongue stroking across her nipple, teasing it as he sucked it further into his mouth. As he continued to suckle at her, his hand slid down her body to the hem of her skirt so that he could draw it up her legs until it pooled around her hips. He removed his mouth from her for long enough to remove her shirt and release the knot at her hip that held her skirt closed. The fabric opened, revealing that she wore nothing beneath, and George groaned, dropping his mouth to her other breast so he could repeat the attention that he had given the first there.

Zsilvia allowed the pressure of his mouth to guide her onto her back and George sat up on his knees so that he could remove his shirt. She struggled to maintain control as he brought the tip of his tongue to her navel and swept it up, tracing a line up the center of her stomach, between her breasts, and along the side of her neck. He blew a cool stream of air onto the trail that he had just created, sending a shiver through her body that settled between her legs and made her writhe against the bed. George rose up over her, straddling her hips so that she was staring at his beautifully chiseled body. She lifted a hand up to run it through the thick dark hair that covered his chest and belly, biting her bottom lip as the coarse strands made the desire surge within her just as it always did. She had never before seen a man with hair on his body and it was something about George that made him even more irresistible to her.

He rested his hand over hers and drew it down to the front of his pants. She could feel his already intense erection pressing through the fabric toward her and she let her hand run along it adoringly. After a few seconds she released the button and eased the zipper down, allowing his cock to spring out into her hand. George's hands cupped her breasts, kneading into them as she stroked him. Fluid collected at the tip and she gathered it with her palm, using it to allow her hand to glide more easily along his length so that she could move at a faster pace.

George groaned and his head fell back, making Zsilvia's stomach clench with even greater need for him. She loved the deep, primal sounds that poured from his body when she touched him. They were at once completely unchained yet kept private only for her to experience. She held him with both hands, cupping him gently with one while she continued her smooth, even strokes with the other. His hips began to rock into her touch, bucking against her as more of the silky fluid slipped across his skin. Finally she couldn't take the temptation any longer and released him with one hand so that she could prop herself up and draw her tongue along the length of his erection.

The taste of him was intoxicating. The more of the sweet-saltiness of him touched her tongue, the more of it she desired and she took him fully into her mouth, letting it fall into the same rhythm as her hand as she savored the feeling of every ridge and vein against her lips and tongue. As she nurtured him with her mouth, she felt George's hand come around his hips so that it could touch her, his finger-tips slipping through her folds to brush against her most sensitive peak. She parted her legs as much as his position would permit her, and tilted her hips into his touch.

George rested his other hand onto the back of her head so that he could guide her into a faster pace, responding with small thrusts of his hips so that he plunged into her throat. After a few moments he gently pulled back, withdrawing from her mouth and easing his hand from between her thighs. He caught her mouth with his and kissed her deeply, entrancing her with the ministration of her tongue with his so that she barely noticed that he was guiding her backwards until she lay on the pillows. His body stretched out over hers so that they touched from their chests down and he continued to kiss her languidly, building her need for him with each tender press of his mouth.

Finally George took his mouth from hers and met her

eyes. Not taking his gaze away from her, he ran his hand down the side of her body and to her leg so that he could catch the back of her thigh and use it to lift her leg up and onto his shoulder. He pressed forward with his body so that her leg came beside her head, opening her up to him fully and allowing him to enter her. Zsilvia moaned as George's impossibly hard cock pressed into her body, causing her to stretch to accommodate him and then tighten around him again so that she cradled him completely within her. Once he settled as deeply inside her as he could get, George paused and Zsilvia closed her eyes so she could savor the feeling of their bodies melding into one another.

She lifted her hands to his face, resting her palms to the curve of his jaw and letting the pads of her thumbs run across his skin tenderly. He turned and touched a kiss to the center of one palm, keeping his mouth close even as he lifted his lips away so that the warmth of his breath rippled down the inside of her wrist. She opened her eyes again and found George gazing at her, focusing on her face as if he were memorizing every delicate lash and the tender bow of her lips. Their eyes melted into each other and he leaned forward, capturing the mouth that she offered up to him and slowly beginning to roll his hips.

His body moved within her as if crafted for that very purpose and Zsilvia struggled to control the emotions that the intense sensations inspired. She moved her hands to his shoulders and then onto his back, holding him close as he shifted so that he could ease her leg off of his shoulder and guide both of them up so that they hooked over his hips and held him firmly. George placed his hands on either side of her ribs and pushed up, giving himself greater leverage, and Zsilvia felt him slide even deeper into her. Her back arched and her fingers dug into his back as a strangled cry escaped her lips.

The feelings were almost overwhelming as soon as he started to move, but she welcomed each deep, intense thrust and allowed her hips to buck slightly with each stroke so that their bodies met. Sweat started to beat on George's forehead as growling sounds poured from his throat. She could feel the muscles in his back shifting beneath his skin, making him feel even more powerful. The beautiful balance of his primal intensity and the tender way that he enveloped her made her feel safe, desired, and loved. It was an incredible combination of burning need and intense seeking of the pleasure he so deeply desired from her, along with a sense that he was reaching into her very being, connecting their hearts and souls as much as their bodies.

His thrusts grew harder and faster, pushing her closer to climax. She tried to hold back, wanting the feeling to last longer, but George's incredible body was irresistible. His groans told her that he was getting close to his peak as well and she let go, crying out as her orgasm washed over her, her body clenching down on him to pull him even deeper within her. George's head fell back and she felt his cock throb as he roared with the climax that hit him. Her body milked him, each of her tremors meeting the pulses that spilled into her.

When the waves ended and her body relaxed, George rested down onto her, kissing along the side of her neck and softly stroking her breast and the side of her ribs with his fingertips. Zsilvia's body hummed with the intense, delicious feeling and she nuzzled closer to his warm, sweaty body. He lowered onto his side and scooped her against him so that her leg draped across his hips and her head tucked into the curve of his neck and shoulder. She listened to his heartbeat, letting the rhythm lull her as it gradually slowed. They breathed in gentle opposition, her filling her lungs as he released his so that their chests and bellies rose and fell with one another and it was as if they exchanged their breath between them.

Zsilvia could think of nothing more perfect than this. She would travel to Earth with her mate, learn of his life there and meet the people who were close to him, and then they would return here so that they could continue building their lives together.

4

Zuri stepped out of the meeting hall and took a breath of the cooler evening air. It had gotten rather close inside with everyone gathering in the banquet hall and for the first time Zuri had realized just how much the compound had grown, if only temporarily, with the humans and Mikana that had joined them. Though their number wasn't a huge addition to those who already lived on the compound, it still seemed tremendously bigger, louder, and more confusing with all of the new faces and voices that filled the space.

Ero had left the hall a few moments before she had and she searched the moonlit open area in front of the hall to see if he was still out there, taking in a few breaths of fresh air like she was. To one side she saw the dark form of her mate hovering at the edge of the center of the compound, his hands on his hips as he paced, occasionally turning toward the forest as if tempted to start running. If he did, there was no way that she would be able to catch up with him.

"Ero?" she called out to him, gathering her skirt in her hands so that she could walk faster across the open area.

Ero looked up at the sound of his name, but then turned and started toward the forest. He wasn't running, but he was walking fast enough that Zuri quickly lost sight of him. She picked up speed, jogging toward the dark edge of the forest and continuing to call out to him. Finally she found him standing in the darkness of the shadows beneath the trees, staring up at the pattern that the branches made across the dark blue night sky.

"I need to get in better shape if I'm ever going to be able to keep up with you," Zuri joked as she walked toward him. "At least you weren't running this time. There's no way I'm ever going to be able to match that."

"You'll never have to."

The darkness in Ero's voice took all of the humor out of Zuri and she stepped toward him, touching her mate's shoulder tenderly.

"What do you mean?"

"I mean I'm never going to run again."

"Ero, running is a part of you. It's something you've always done. It's one of the first things that I found out about you. What do you mean you aren't ever going to do it again?"

Ero shook his head and turned away from her, the movement shaking her hand away from him. She allowed it to lower to her side, not wanting to upset him any further than he already was. He had seemed fine when they were in the banquet hall, laughing and talking with the others as they planned their trip to Earth, but now it seemed like all of the light that was in him had been drawn out and he was an empty shell standing just feet from her.

"You heard why I'm able to run as fast as I am," he said, his voice dropping even further.

"You can run fast because you were born to. It's something special about you that sets you apart from all of the other Denynso."

Ero gave a mirthless laugh and turned so that his back was completely to her.

"It's not something special about me. It sets me apart because I'm not like the others. As if I hadn't been reminded of that my entire life, now I know that I am even less a part of them than I ever thought."

"That's not true, Ero," Zuri said, trying to comfort him with the sound of her voice now that he had stepped away from her touch. "You are just as much a part of them as they are a part of you."

"I'm part Klimnu, Zuri," Ero shouted.

The sentence came out of him explosively, harshly as if he had been fighting putting a voice to what he had been thinking. He whipped around as he said it and Zuri could see the pain and fury mingled in his eyes even in the faint glow from the moonlight. She knew her mate's eyes. She knew the rich orange color that they had assumed as soon as they had completed their bond as a way of showing anyone else who looked at him that he had found his life-long mate and was linked to her for the rest of his life. She knew the light in them that usually sparkled and danced even when he was just talking with her as if there was so much energy and life inside him that it couldn't stay calm. That light wasn't there now. The happiness had been dampened out of him and it made her ache.

"I know," she said, not knowing what else to say.

The revelation from Creia that generations ago two Denynso women gave birth to children who were half other species was shocking, but it was even harder when he continued on to tell them that one of those children was the progeny of a Klimnu. It had disturbed Ero deeply when he learned the closely-held secret of his ancestry. He had always felt like an outsider in his own clan. An orphan from the time he was just a young child, Ero was far smaller and less powerful than the other warriors of the clan. Though he had been adopted by Creia and Theia, the position of his new parents had done nothing to ease the pain and struggle that he had been through. It had merely put him in even closer contact with the biggest and strongest warriors, growing up with them as his brothers.

This meant that he grew up with an even greater sense of inferiority, tormented by his adopted brothers for being smaller, weaker, and less aggressive. It was this lifelong torment that had nearly cost him the love of Zuri, who he turned on and made fun of cruelly because of her size. Though he hadn't shown any of the sense of self-hatred and self-consciousness since he had come to Earth to bring her back, the revelation that his smaller size and the incredible speed that he could maintain when he ran came from Klimnu heritage emerging after decades of being hidden seemed to have drawn out all of these painful feelings again and now he was suffering. Zuri hated to see the pain and self-doubt in his eyes, but she didn't know what she could do to ease it.

"How could I ever want to run again when I now know that the only reason that I can do it is because of the Klimnu? I can't believe I was so stupid as to never make the connection. They were always so fast when we fought them. I thought that being able to move as fast as them was an advantage. I could take them out more easily because I could keep up with them in a way that the other warriors couldn't. Now I know that the only reason that was possible is because I was using the same heritage as they were."

"Why does that have to be something that you hate, Ero? I know that the Klimnu have been the greatest enemy of the Denynso, but hasn't everything that has happened in the last few weeks taught you anything?"

"What could it have possibly taught me other than to hate the Klimnu even more? They destroyed the planet that they took over when they left Uoria, and then they burned the entire Denynso compound to the ground, killing all of them. This all happened even before they decided to wage war against our half of the clan."

"Do you know what I see when I look at you, Ero?"

Ero looked at her, his jaw twitching slightly.

"What?"

Zuri stepped up to him and rested her hands on his cheeks.

"I don't see Klimnu. I see the beauty, the kindness, and the intelligence of the Mikana."

"They were beautiful when they caused the volcanoes to erupt and burned the other Denynso compound."

"And they're beautiful now. Don't forget that we know some of the Mikana. You know Maxim and Rey. Do you see Klimnu in them?"

Ero hesitated for a few seconds.

"No. But the potential is there, Zuri. You know that. You saw Maxim change just like I did."

"And I also saw him healed, and I see the way that he looks at Ivy. I don't see evil there. I see love and tenderness and strength, just like I see when I look at you. Sure the potential to become Klimnu is in him just like it was in every single one of the Mikana that lived at the time of the split. The difference is that most of them chose not to let greed, darkness, fear, and hatred take over them. Most of them remained hopeful, led by their intelligence and by the beauty within them."

"But the man I come from was part of the Klimnu."

"Because he was born into it. He wasn't one of the men who separated from the group. He was born into the family, but what if just like the potential to become Klimnu existed in all of the Mikana, the potential to be Mikana existed in all of the Klimnu? What if he chose to be led by that part of him?"

"How can I know that?"

"Does it matter? You have within you the ability to choose just like every one of them did. You can choose to hate the part of yourself that could be led by darkness and hatred, or you could choose to embrace the part of you that is strong enough to overcome the power of that darkness even in the face of adversity."

5

"**A**re you sure that you don't want to come along with us?"

Creia looked at Gyyx, the bright orange eyes of the young warrior making something inside him feel even more painful than it already did, and shook his head. He tried to smile, but he wasn't sure if the expression was actually come across on his lips.

"No. As wonderful as it sounds to visit Earth and see what it's like outside of Uoria, my responsibilities are here. Someone has to be here in order to take care of the compound and those who aren't leaving, and to make sure that if any emergencies arise they can get handled as quickly and effectively as possible. "

"It won't be the same without you, though. We already left the compound for the first time without you. We shouldn't be leaving the planet for the first time without our king."

"Don't you worry," Creia said, resting his hand on Gyyx's shoulder to try to calm his protests, "there will be plenty more opportunities to travel and I fully intend that one of these days I am going to be on one of those shuttles to Earth and these women can show me some of the things that they carry on about. This time, though, my warriors are just going to have to be strong and carry on without me."

"You'll miss Ty's wedding."

"I don't even know what a wedding is Gyyx," Creia said, finally able to muster a soft laugh.

"I know, but it seems that it's something that you should be there for."

"Gyyx, there are decisions to be made and wounds to heal. Right now is not the time for the compound to be without its king. As much as I would like to be there to witness whatever this ritual is that Samira has convinced Ty to undergo, and that I suspect a few of the other warriors will fall into place doing as well, I have to think of my responsibilities and my role here first. There are others who are leaving the compound in the morning and I have to make sure that I am here for them when they return. As for now, you should be making your preparations to leave and that starts with getting your mate home so that she can get some rest. She looks asleep on her feet." Gyyx glanced down at Leia who was leaning on his arm with her eyes nearly closed. She was a tiny, delicate creature and sometimes it still startled Creia to see her with Gyyx, but the two were incredibly passionate about each other, devoted in a way that warmed his heart each time he saw them, especially when he thought of the horrific experiences that Leia had to endure just to get to where she was. "Go on, Gyyx," he said. "Go home and start getting ready for your journey."

Not looking convinced, but knowing that he was fairly well out of arguments, Gyyx swept Leia up into his arms, cradled her against his chest, and started out of the nearly empty hall. All that was left at the tables was two of the humans that Creia recognized as being members of the settlement that the warriors had released from the bonds of the Covra and the two warriors who were acting as their guardians though Creia had made no formal proclamation that those who were visiting from the other locations needed such guards.

As Gyyx disappeared through the main door of the building Creia felt his mate's hand rest on his shoulder. He glanced back to look at her and saw the knowing look in her eyes.

"What are you really thinking about, Creia?" she asked.

"What do you mean?"

He knew exactly what Theia meant, but he figured that he could delay answering, giving himself more time without having to put a voice to what was really happening in his mind. Finally the four men at the last table stood and made their way toward the door to the hall. They turned back to wish him goodnight and he waved at them, watching until the door closed behind them.

"I know you, Creia. You may be able to convince Gyyx that you want to stay behind here just so that you can hold down the fort while everyone is gone, but I know that isn't true. Something is bothering you and you are just waiting for that shuttle to leave for Earth for you to be able to do something about it. What is it?"

"I meant what I said to Gyyx, Theia. My first responsibility, as it always has been, is to the compound. I can't leave it without its rulers while the warriors are gone either on a completely different planet or on the other side of this one. If there is one thing that we've learned in the last few weeks it is that we never know what's going to happen. We can't assume that everything's going to be ok and that the compound is going to be secure. I can't leave it knowing that at any moment there could be another threat that comes and invades. This is our home and I can't put it at risk by leaving it."

"I understand that, and I agree with you. With things as fragile as they are right now, leaving the compound without any leadership or protection would be a terrible idea. But I also know that that isn't the only thing that is on your mind right now. You could easily assign one of the warriors who plans on going to the settlement to stay with me, or arrange for a shuttle that will bring you there and back in as short a time as possible without having to travel with the others, but you didn't."

Creia stared at his mate for several long, tense seconds, and then stepped down from the platform, stalking toward the back of the hall to the large tapestry that covered the curved stairwell to their living quarters. He didn't want to be in the hall any longer. He needed the privacy of his own space so that he could feel safe, so that he could relax out of the leadership role that he always had to take, and the tension that he had been feeling around his people since they returned from their quest across the planet. He had always tried to rule in a different way than the kings of his childhood. They had been far more distant from the people of the clan, avoiding meeting with them personally and maintaining a sense of formality with them that made them highly respected and formidable leaders, but made it so that they lacked the warmth that he wanted to offer the members of the clan when he stepped into the role of king. In choosing to rule this way, however, he had allowed himself to become far more attached to the individuals of the clan, caring for them well beyond the traditional responsibilities and relationships of a king to his subjects. While this had allowed him to enjoy what amounted to a tremendous extended family and a much greater sense of love and connection than had existed in his time with his own king, it also meant that he experienced a level of pain, fear, and disappointment that he didn't believe his king ever would have felt.

At the top of the stairs Creia released the latch at the front of the cloak he wore and let it fall from his shoulders. Theia was close behind him and scooped it up before it even touched the floor. After being bonded for decades, they existed in an easy and comfortable pattern that allowed them to predict each other in a way that was peaceful and comfortable, even if some of his habits were frustrating to his queen.

"Creia, how many times..."

"I failed them, Theia."

Creia cut her off, the words coming out of him like he could no longer hold them inside and it was as if they took all of the energy out of his body as they emerged. He sank down onto one of the large circular cushions in the center of the room and hung his face into his hands. He could feel Theia cross the room slowly and lower herself onto the chair in front of the cushion. She sat silently for several long seconds, giving Creia time to process what he was thinking and feeling before she reached forward and rested her hand on his head, gently stroking his hair back from his forehead.

"Who did you fail?"

"All of them," Creia said mournfully without lifting his head up out of his hands. "I've always thought that my greatest responsibility was to protect them and the compound, and so I hid things from them that I never should have hidden. I kept them within the compound borders and let all of the danger and the threats come to them rather than allowing them to venture out and find the dangers for themselves."

"But they defeated them, Creia," Theia soothed, sliding down off of the edge of the seat so that she could sink down onto her knees and pull Creia's face into her hands. "When the dangers came, your warriors were ready. They were able to protect the compound and the entirety of the clan."

"But they never should have been here. I never should have allowed the enemies to come into our compound and put the women at risk."

"The women are more than capable of taking care of themselves, as has been proven to us over the last few weeks."

"The warriors fought without ever knowing really why they were fighting. They knew that they had built a reputation of being fearsome warriors, but they didn't know why, and they didn't know why the other species would want to come here. I kept all of that from them."

"Even you don't know everything. You don't know why some of them came, but you do know why they stayed away, and that's because of the warriors."

"But they came because of a history that I never shared with them. They came because they knew of the wars with the Covra, the Klimnu, and the Valdicians. How do we know that some of them hadn't built alliances with those species and have been trying to carry on those wars all this time? I feel responsible for all of the pain and heartache that those men and their mates have had to go through because I didn't take care of them like I should have. I let them go off into areas of the planet where they had never been and that I didn't prepare them to experience. I didn't give them the warnings that I should have given them."

"What could you have warned them about? You didn't

know what the Covra had done any more than they did, and you didn't know that the Mikana still existed. You closed yourself off from the world as much as you closed them off. They wanted to go out of the compound and find out what else could be threatening us. All you did was honor those wishes and allow them to go. There was nothing more that you could do."

"I knew about the species that went underground, Theia. I knew that they existed before the Denynso moved onto this compound."

"Did you know that there were still there?"

Theia's voice carried a hint of the betrayal that Creia had never wanted to hear coming from her. Even worse than the thought that he had failed the rest of the clan was the thought that he had betrayed and disappointed his mate.

"I didn't. I wasn't even completely positive that they had gone beneath the same ground. We never fully knew what happened to them. I didn't know that they were right beneath us."

"When did you figure it out?"

Creia sighed. He hated admitting any of this to Theia, but he knew that he had to. He no longer had the choice to stay silent. It had caused too much pain already.

"I began to suspect it when the women went down into that tunnel and found the section that transported them down into the cavern. There would be no reason for that type of technology to exist if there wasn't a species that was going to utilize it regularly. It occurred to me that it might be there to help people who lived down there be able to get around more quickly without being detected. But it is not the type of technology that their kind created. That is from another kind, so I convinced myself that it wasn't the people who had lived here and were driven underground by the Covra and the Valdicians."

"What were that species called? Who were they?"

Creia looked into his mate's eyes and shook his head. He felt uncharacteristic tears building in his own eyes, but he didn't bother to fight them or even to wipe them away as they started down his cheeks.

"I don't know," he whispered. "I don't remember who they were or what they were called. We never even asked Loralia. She is the last of her kind and I never even asked her what that kind was."

The realization ached within him as Creia let the realization that if it hadn't been for the war with the Klimnu that brought his warriors down into the cavern, an entire species would have been lost and would be forgotten forever. He wondered if he could have done anything. If he could have figured out that they were down there, was there anything that he could have done that might have saved them from the horrific plague that killed so many only to return later and destroy all but one of their once prolific and strong number?

He knew that he had not done what he needed to do, what he had been entrusted to do when he was chosen as king, and it was time to rectify it.

6

———

Leia sat in the corner of the living room, her knees pulled up toward her chest so that she could use her thighs as a support for her sketchpad. The pencil balanced in her hand like an extension of herself and when the tip touched the paper and the lines began to form on the creamy surface it was like the embodiment of her breath. It had been that way since she had first begun to draw and discovered that those lines, those tangible versions of her thoughts and emotions, were the most effective way that she could express herself. It was through these lines that she could explore the pain and confusion that defined her life while keeping her safe. No one knew what she was thinking when she drew, and even when her pieces were complete, those who looked at them weren't able to interpret them as anything more than the shapes and objects that they could see.

She was feeling that way again now, tucked away from everything and existing only in that corner through the pencil and paper she held. Her hand was shaking as she drew and she couldn't completely focus on what the lines were going to become, but what mattered was that she was making them. Just that small amount of control gave her comfort and peace. She could hear the sound of a door opening and closing above her and she knew that Gyyx had finished with his shower and was making his way toward the bedroom. Her mate would expect her to be waiting for him in bed, but she hadn't been able to sleep. When she laid down and closed her eyes, all she could see was the cold, wet walls of the prison.

"Leia?"

Gyyx's voice came down the staircase at her and she felt it wash over her comfortingly. Even if she needed to retreat to the security of the corner and her sketchpad sometimes, simply hearing her mate's voice could make her feel safe and secure. When she didn't call back out to him, Gyyx started down the stairs toward her and by the speed of the sound of his footsteps she could tell that he was worried about her. It had been quite a while since the last time that drawing had been a salvation rather than just something that she enjoyed doing, and just as long since she saw the prison walls when she closed her eyes. Now, though, she feared even blinking because she worried that the next time she saw those walls she would also see Klimnu that held her within them.

"Are you alright?" he asked, lowering his tremendous body down to sit beside her on the floor.

The presence of him on the floor with her was as powerful as his voice and she started to feel her body pulling out of the corner toward him. No longer did she feel like she had to find her protection by retreating. If Gyyx was near her, she felt like she was protected.

"I think that everything just got to be too much," she said.

"Are you seeing them again?" he asked.

She could hear the concern in his voice. There was a time in her life when any type of emotion like that would have frightened her, making her feel like she was going to suffer serious repercussions for causing anything unpleasant. She would have struggled to apologize, to explain away how she was feeling, and to make the other person forget. Gyyx, however, had taught her that she didn't have to feel that way. He always allowed her to feel any way that she was going to, and simply let her know that he was there to hold her up.

"I haven't in so long, but then knowing that you were there, that you saw it again..."

Her voice trailed off and Gyyx nodded. She knew that she didn't need to say anything else. He understood exactly what she meant without her having to give any more words to it. She had stayed behind at the compound with Eden while the other women had left with George to help the men at the settlement. It had hurt her that she had not been able to reconnect with her mate the way that the other women had, but at the very end of a pregnancy that had already been tense and frighteningly filled with a sense of the unknown, Eden couldn't have been left alone. She had formed a close bond with the pretty scientist and it seemed only right that she be the one who would stay behind and take care of her. She had been overjoyed to see Gyyx again when they returned to the compound, but soon she realized that his return was not the happy occasion that she had wanted it to be. Instead, the return was filled with darkness that brought up memories so painful they took Leia's breath away.

Leia hated that Gyyx had seen what was left of the prison again. Even though she hadn't been there, she had for a few moments before he closed them off his thoughts to her, the thoughts that he was having as he stared down at the remnants of the destroyed building. She knew that he felt an indescribable level of anger and sorrow when he stood on that land and looked down at the blackened, skeletal remains of the foundation and the subterranean floors of the building. It was there that the Klimnu had brought her after taking over the shuttle that she was riding to Uoria. They had tortured and tormented her, keeping her in a tiny, grimy cell for nearly two months before she managed to escape and was discovered near death in the middle of a hallway by Elianna.

The battle that had broken out at the prison that night had been like nothing she had ever experienced. Though she only remembered brief slivers of it, moments like the few seconds of illumination in a flash of lightning, she distinctly remembered the intensity. She later learned the details of it and found out that the Denynso warriors, these men who she had come to the planet to draw, had fought the Klimnu bravely and burned their prison to the ground, destroying as much of it as they thought existed. They hadn't known about the basement rooms, however. They didn't know that she remembered them distinctly from the few but horrible times she had been taken out of her cell and brought down there.

Even worse than hearing about the prison again and finding out the grisly history of the building, starting with the fact that it had not, in fact, been built by the design of the Klimnu, but by the design and desire of the Covra and the hands of the Mikana, was hearing the extent to which Pyra had changed during the journey and the bloodthirsty way he was treating the Mikana. She knew what they were. She knew what had happened to the young man named

Maxim who had proven to them that the Klimnu still lived but in the beautiful, kind form that had existed so long before. But even she had been able to see past that when she looked at Maxim and Rey and not think of them as the brutal creatures that had held her captive for so long. When she looked at these two beautiful men she could still see the stains of the blood of their ancestors on their hands and had even felt a pang of compassion for them. There was something strangely poetic about being enslaved and forced to build something horrible, only generations later to have the descendants of those who suffered reclaim the space, even if for their own cruelty.

There was nothing poetic or understandable about Pyra's behavior, however. She couldn't justify what he had done and even though in his mind his determination to kill off all of the Mikana had been as a source of protection for the rest of the compound, Leia could only see it as a start and painful reminder of what she had gone through. He hated without limitation and without qualification. By merit only of being born into the same species as a group of rogue extremists who caused widespread pain and panic, these men would have to die, just as the Klimnu hadn't cared who she was or what her intentions on the planet were after she arrived. They only cared that she was human and that she was going to be in contact with the Denynso.

"Are you looking forward to going back to Earth?" Gyyx asked her.

The question shook her out of her thoughts and helped her to draw her focus away from the darkness within her.

"I think so," she replied.

In truth, she hadn't really thought much about what going back to Earth meant or what she might encounter when she was there. She had been so lost in everything that was happening around her, and the thoughts that were tormenting her as she tried to make sense out of everything that had been learned on the journey that it still hadn't really sunken in that in just a matter of days she would be getting back onto a shuttle and heading to the planet that for 57 days of captivity she thought she would never see again, and then since bonding with Gyyx never really wanted to see again.

"Is there anything that you want to do while you're there?" he asked.

Leia knew that Gyyx understood her past. It had been a brutally difficult conversation that they had had to have extremely early in their relationship, but one that was absolutely integral to their ability to come together and share their lives. Gyyx knew that there was little on Earth that she actually cared about, and even less that she would ever want to see or do again, but at the same time, she couldn't forget completely who she was before she had found him.

"I want to see Samira get married," she answered. "Never in my life have I known a happily married couple that stayed happily married for more than a few weeks. I want to be able to see that from the beginning and I know that they will be happy together for the rest of their lives. I'd also like to show you where I grew up."

"Are you sure?" Gyyx asked, sounding surprised that she would want to revisit those painful memories.

Leia nodded. She looked back down at her sketchpad and realized that she had continued to draw even as they spoke. The smooth page was now covered in a weaving, knotted vine studded with lethally pointed thorns.

"I feel like I need to see it again now that I have you. I want to face it. It still has power over me and I can't stand that. I feel like if I can see it again, if I can walk into those places that are such dark, looming forces in my life but I can have you with me, I can take away the power that they have and I can really move on."

"Then I'm willing to go anywhere that you need me to go," Gyyx said, pushing himself up from the floor and reaching down for her. "Now let's get to bed. The others are leaving early in the morning and I want to be able to be there to send them off."

Leia placed her sketchpad and pencil on the floor beside her and rested her hands in Gyyx's. They were so small compared to his, but that only made her feel safer. He could fully envelope her, completely surround her so that nothing else in the world could get close to her. With him, in him, she was safe.

"I still feel like I should go with you."

Lynx reached out and took the canvas bag from Ciyrs' hand and slung it over his shoulder to join his own bag.

"No," said Lynx simply. "You go with the others to Earth and enjoy the wedding. We're going to be fine. We're just going to free the captives, pack up some of the belongings, and bring people back here. There aren't going to be any battles this time."

"We didn't think that there were going to be any battles before," the healer protested. "What happens if the Covra aren't really gone or the Mikana are combative when they're released?"

"They won't be combative," Maxim said.

Lynx nodded toward the young man and then look at Ciyrs.

"See? From the lips of one of them himself, the Mikana won't be combative. This isn't like the first time. We aren't there to imprison them or to question them. We're there to let them go. That's all. If they want to come back to the compound and work with the rest of us to start rebuilding positive relations, that's great. If they want to go back to their kingdom and go about their lives, that's great, too. They have the choice. They won't have any reason to be combative."

"What if someone gets sick or injured?"

Lynx patted the bag that he had taken from Ciyrs.

"You packed enough supplies that we will be able to handle it. We have Rey with us, and as he showed us on the top of those rocks, he has some skills when it comes to taking care of people who need it."

"He helped deliver a baby. He didn't handle an injury or an illness or a war wound."

Lynx reached out and took his friend by the shoulders.

"We are going to be fine," he said.

Ciyrs still didn't look convinced. This was an uncomfortable situation for all of them. They were not accustomed to the clan splitting off into so many directions. Their time in the settlement when Pyra led the small group to the kingdom where they encountered the Mikana was the first time that they had purposely divided for more than a few hours, and now they were planning not just to divide, but for several of them to go to a completely new and unknown to them planet while the others stayed behind and returned to the site that had been the center of all of the turmoil that they had experienced. Lynx understood what they were dealing with, but he also knew that it was important that each of them went where he was needed, and even though the warriors and their mates were planning on going to Earth for a wedding, Lynx felt deep in his gut that what they would encounter on earth had the potential to be much more challenging than what he was going to encounter back at the settlement. It was far more likely that they would need the healer, though Lynx hoped with everything in him that they wouldn't.

"Is everyone ready to go?"

They all turned to see Creia approaching from across the clearing in front of the meeting hall. He had the same warm, proud smile on his face that he carried most of the time, but Lynx could see new signs of age wearing on his face. The last several weeks had impacted him just as it had impacted the rest, but it seemed to be especially hard on their king. He knew that it had to have been extremely difficult for Creia to admit that he hadn't been completely forthcoming with the clan, and to show them the ever-burning remnants of the old compound that he had held as a torturing secret within himself for the entire time that he had been king.

Around Lynx the rest of the group that was traveling back to the settlement called out their affirmations and Creia nodded. He stopped a few feet away from them and looked at each, his eyes lingering on their faces for a few moments before he gave a short nod.

"This time you are facing something even more than you faced the first time. The dangers may no longer be there, but the damage that they left in their wake is. It is your responsibility now to start repairing that damage. We all have to come together now, and that starts with just one person taking a step forward and closing the space between us." He reached into one of the deep pockets of the tunic that he wore and held out a rolled piece of parchment toward Lynx. "This is my official proclamation releasing the Mikana and restoring their absolute sovereignty over their kingdom and their own kind. It never should have been threatened. Please carry this and my apologies back to them. Let them know that they are welcome here and that I look forward to working toward making new connections and building a new and cooperative relationship with them."

Lynx nodded and tucked the parchment into his bag. He felt the tremendous sense of responsibility on him. He had been chosen to lead this group, building off of both the assignment that Pyra had given him when they were in the settlement and the trust that his leadership had inspired in the rest of them. Though none of them had voiced it in those exact words, there was a great sense of relief when he had told the group that he and Rain decided to go with them rather than going to Earth with the others. It seemed that having him as well as a leading member of the Nyx 23 humans and the Mikana created a mutually cooperative balance within the group that allowed them to feel like a united force as they started into this new chapter together.

Creia stepped back and allowed the others who were gathered behind him to step forward so that they could say their goodbyes to the group. Ty was the first to approach Lynx. He reached out and took his friend's hand, feeling a twinge of guilt in his stomach as he looked into the gentle baker's eyes.

"I'm sorry that I'm not going to be there for your wedding," Lynx said.

Ty shook his head with a soft smile.

"You're doing what you have to do," he said. "As much as I would like all of my warrior brothers there with me, I know that there is still so much to be done here and I feel better knowing that you are here to make sure that it gets done."

"I can't do it all."

"No," Ty agreed, "but you can make those first steps that Creia was talking about. You can be the one that starts building the bridges between all of us. Besides, you are just staying here and going where we've all gone before. I get to go to Earth."

Lynx laughed at the childlike excitement in Ty's voice. Visiting Earth had been something that they had all talked about and wondered about when they were younger. It seemed like such a distant dream to visit the huge and complex planet that had for so long been considered the center of the universe. Without technology to travel off of the planet, however, it had seemed like it would never happen, and even when the humans started to visit with frequency, the thought of the Denynso being able to simply climb aboard one of the shuttles and visit a planet where none of their kind had ever stepped seemed out of the realm of reality. Now it was not only possible, but imminent and the excitement among those who were going on the journey was palpable.

Ty stepped away to go talk to others in the group and Lynx leaned down to kiss Samira on the cheek. Pyra stepped up to him and pulled Lynx in for a hug.

"I'm proud of you," Pyra said in a voice low enough that only Lynx could hear it. "I know that you will be the leader that I wasn't able to be."

The sentiment sent a pain through Lynx's heart. He hated to hear Pyra, the man who he had admired for his entire life, talk that way about himself.

"You have always been an amazing leader, Pyra," Lynx told him. "You have led us through all of our battles and you will continue to lead us through whatever we face in the future."

Pyra was shaking his head as he stepped back.

"I wasn't the leader that any of you needed, but you were. You will be strong for them and they will follow you because you earned their trust. I will continue to work to earn the trust that I once had back."

"You will, Pyra."

Lynx stepped back toward Rain and took her hand. He looked over his shoulder at the rest of the people traveling with him and let out a long breath before turning back to the group that was staying behind.

"Safe travels to all of you," he said. "We'll see you when you return from Earth. For those of you who won't be returning to Uoria, I am glad to have met all of you and I'm happy that you're getting to return home. I know that it won't be easy for you, but I hope that you find the happiness there that you've been missing. Remember that you will always be a part of Uoria and that you will always have an ally in the Denynso."

Rain squeezed his hand and Lynx returned the gesture. He looked into the faces of each of the people standing in front of him for a few more seconds and then turned, starting across the compound toward the forest. The dark edge of the trees had always seemed mysterious to him when he was younger. He had known that the far boundary of the compound was beyond those trees and he had always known that he wasn't to even approach the boundary much less go beyond it. Now the trees were only a part of the journey, a peaceful section of the long walk that would bring them beyond the boundary and out onto the planet that was just now showing its secrets to them.

8

The banquet hall felt empty and quiet now that so many of the warriors were missing. Even though their number had been replaced by the humans and the Mikana who were still with them, the presence of the warriors was so strong that being without it made the space feel strangely abandoned. Zuri hadn't visited the hall for meals during the time that the men had been on their quest, preferring instead to eat with the other women in their homes so that they didn't have to face the continuous reminder of their mates being away from the compound. Now that they had returned, however, the clan wanted to gather in the hall as they always did so that they could eat together and continue with their preparations for their journey.

The long wooden table in front of her was empty, reminding her of the group that had stayed behind at the settlement and those who had left the day before to return to them. The table where she sat, however, was filled with the warriors and their mates who were preparing to travel when the shuttle came in two days. She could feel the tension that they were feeling even beneath the excitement. She and the other women had been doing their best to comfort the warriors, to explain to them what it would be like to travel on the shuttles. Zuri thought back to the first time she rode the shuttle to Uoria and how she had felt during the trip. It was a strange experience, but one that she was always happy she had taken.

"How many shuttles are coming?" Bannack asked.

"Creia said that there would be at least two. The university tried to arrange for two of the newest shuttles. They accommodate more passengers and are faster, but he hasn't heard from them since the planned day of dispatch so I guess we won't know until they show up," Samira said.

"Have any of you traveled on the new shuttles?" Ciyrs asked.

The women shook their heads.

"The only one of us who has is Ivy."

"And she's not here."

"No."

"You're going to be fine," Zuri said, offering a small smile to Bannack. "The trip is really no big deal. You can have them sedate you if you want them to."

"Sedate us?"

Zuri nodded. She remembered that experience strongly. During her first five-day journey to Uoria she had rejected the service from the attendant that would allow her to sleep contained within her passenger pod from soon after take-off until just before their arrival. She wanted to stay awake for the experience and use the time to prepare for what she thought was going to be a few months of participation as a visiting professor in the university exchange program with the Denynso.

"They can put you to sleep so that you don't even realize

that the trip is happening. It makes it go by much faster and you don't even really have the time to be nervous about traveling. You get into your pod, they start the process, and the next thing you know they are waking you up to prepare for arrival."

Zuri tried not to think about why she remembered that experience. She didn't ever want to revisit those awful days after Ero had been so cruel to her that she insisted on leaving Uoria to return to Earth on the same shuttle that had brought her, less than 24 hours after she had arrived. During that trip she hadn't wanted to be able to think. She hadn't wanted to hear his voice repeating through her head. Instead, she rested back into the passenger pod, closed her eyes, and let the sedation take over.

"What about once we get there?" Bannack asked.

She could hear a hint of nervousness in his voice that he was trying hard to cover. The courage of the Denynso was legendary and the warriors never liked to show vulnerability away from private moments with their mates.

"What do you mean?" Zuri asked.

"No Denynso has ever traveled to Earth. What are they going to think of us?"

"That's not true." Zuri turned to Ero. He had been silent the entire time they were in the banquet hall and had spoken very little since their conversation in the forest. "I've been."

The warriors looked at him, the looks in their eyes saying that they had forgotten that Ero had once visited Earth. It had been such a brief, spontaneous trip that many of them hadn't even thought of it.

"You have," Zuri said softly, reaching to take her mate's hand. "Ero came to Earth to get me after I left. He traveled completely on his own and he made his way from the university to my house without any help."

"If it hadn't been for such an unpleasant reason, I would have really enjoyed the trip," Ero said, lifting his eyes to look at the rest of the warriors. "As for Earth itself, I only encountered one real problem."

"What was that?" Ciyrs asked.

Zuri saw Ero's eyes slide over to Samira as he wordlessly asked her permission to tell them. He knew exactly what he was thinking about, and she felt uncomfortable even without the words having been spoken. Samira nodded.

"It's alright, Ero," she said. "You can talk about it."

"Samira's stepfather," Ero said. "He was absolute vermin. You can't blame that on the entirety of Earth, however. He was just one person. Remember that Samira, Zuri, Eden, Leia, Elianna, George, Ivy, Rain, and the rest of Nyx 23 are all from Earth. That is far more people that have fully accepted us than the one who was cruel."

"And he wasn't cruel to Ero because he is Denynso," Samira explained. "He is just a horrible, vicious human being. He has never been truly kind to another living thing."

"You have to remember," Eden said, tenderly adjusting Lysander over her shoulder and patting him, "Earth is not sparse like Uoria. There are many different species that live or visit there. There aren't as many as there are humans, but there are enough that it won't seem unusual for you to be there. I would even venture to say that there are some people who will be excited to finally have the Denynso on Earth."

"Really?" Bannack asked.

"Absolutely," Zuri said. "The university was extremely excited to start the exchange program, and there have been humans visiting here for quite some time. Earth is curious about the Denynso and most are eager to find out more. If anything, you might find that they are a bit too excited to meet you."

Zuri laughed as Ero pressed in closer to her. She knew that the warriors who were mated would have no interest in the human women who would inevitably find them attractive, and that if any of those women got too close to them, they would experience the searing heat that radiated off of the men's skin to keep such unwanted attention away from them. The single warriors, however, would likely have more than enough available women to choose from, and she was sure that they would leave a trail of heartbreak in their wake.

She looked over at Ero and he met her eyes. The pain that was there when they were in the forest was still there, but it was softer now, veiled by something more, something that told her that he was beginning to understand what she had said to him about his heritage and that maybe, someday soon, he would run again.

TBC

(To be continued in book III...)